D1017056

The Big, Big Wall

The Big, Big Wall

Reginald Howard
Illustrated by Ariane Dewey and
Jose Aruego

Green Light Readers
Harcourt, Inc.
Orlando   Austin   New York   San Diego   Toronto   London

Humpty Dumpty sat on a wall.

He did not want to have a big fall.

One friend came to the big, big wall.

"I will help you. You will not fall."

"Oh, not you. You look too small."

Two friends came to the big, big wall.

"We will help you. You will not fall."

"Oh, not you. You look too small."

Three friends came to the big, big wall.

"We will all help you. You will not fall."

Humpty Dumpty smiled at his friends.

"Now I can come back down again."

Walk With Me

Humpty Dumpty's friends worked together to help him get down from the wall. Work together with a friend in this game.

1 Stand beside your friend.

2 Tie one of your legs to one of your friend's legs.

3 Try walking or hopping.

What happens?
What did you learn about working together?

Meet the Illustrators

Ariane Dewey has lots of rabbits visit her yard. She loves to watch them nibble dandelions. Ariane thought about those rabbits as she painted the rabbit in *The Big, Big Wall*. She says that cheery colors make her feel good. She hopes her purple rabbit and colorful animals make you happy, too.

Ariane Dewey

Jose Aruego had a pet pig named Snort when he was young. "I loved that pig!" Jose says. "He was so soft and funny." When Jose had to find a way to keep Humpty Dumpty from having a big fall, he thought about Snort. He decided that a pig would be a great cushion for Humpty Dumpty!

Jose Aruego

For information about permission to reproduce selections from this book, please write
to Permissions, Houghton Mifflin Harcourt Publishing Company
215 Park Avenue South NY, NY 10003.

www.hmhco.com

First Green Light Readers edition 2001
Green Light Readers is a trademark of Harcourt, Inc., registered in the
United States of America and/or other jurisdictions.

The Library of Congress has cataloged an earlier edition as follows:
Howard, Reginald.
The big, big wall/by Reginald Howard; illustrated by Jose Aruego and
Ariane Dewey.
p. cm.
"Green Light Readers."
Summary: Humpty Dumpty's friends help him avoid a big, big fall.
[1. Eggs—Fiction. 2. Friendship—Fiction. 3. Stories in rhyme.]
I. Aruego, Jose, ill. II. Dewey, Ariane, ill. III. Title. IV. Green Light reader.
PZ8.3.H825Bi 2001
[E]—dc21   00-9724
ISBN 0-15-204813-8
ISBN 0-15-204853-7 (pb)

SCP 10 9
4500519556

Ages 4-6
Grades: K-1
Guided Reading Level: C-D
Reading Recovery Level: 6-7

Green Light Readers
For the reader who's ready to GO!

"A must-have for any family with a beginning reader."—*Boston Sunday Herald*

"You can't go wrong with adding several copies of these terrific books to your beginning-to-read collection."—*School Library Journal*

"A winner for the beginner."—*Booklist*

Five Tips to Help Your Child Become a Great Reader

1. Get involved. Reading aloud to and with your child is just as important as encouraging your child to read independently.

2. Be curious. Ask questions about what your child is reading.

3. Make reading fun. Allow your child to pick books on subjects that interest her or him.

4. Words are everywhere—not just in books. Practice reading signs, packages, and cereal boxes with your child.

5. Set a good example. Make sure your child sees YOU reading.

Why Green Light Readers Is the Best Series for Your New Reader

- Created exclusively for beginning readers by some of the biggest and brightest names in children's books

- Reinforces the reading skills your child is learning in school

- Encourages children to read—and finish—books by themselves

- Offers extra enrichment through fun, age-appropriate activities unique to each story

- Incorporates characteristics of the Reading Recovery program used by educators

- Developed with Harcourt School Publishers and credentialed educational consultants